Kipper and Roly

Other Kipper Books

<table>
<tr><td>Kipper</td><td>Kipper's Book of Weather</td></tr>
<tr><td>Kipper's A to Z: An Alphabet Adventure</td><td>Kipper Has a Party (Sticker Story)</td></tr>
<tr><td>Kipper's Birthday</td><td>Kipper in the Snow (Sticker Story)</td></tr>
<tr><td>Kipper's Christmas Eve</td><td>Kipper and the Egg (Touch and Feel)</td></tr>
<tr><td>Kipper's Monster</td><td>Kipper's Kite (Touch and Feel)</td></tr>
<tr><td>Kipper's Snowy Day</td><td>Kipper's Sticky Paws (Touch and Feel)</td></tr>
<tr><td>Kipper's Toybox</td><td>Kipper's Surprise (Touch and Feel)</td></tr>
<tr><td>Where, Oh Where, Is Kipper's Bear?</td><td>Kipper's Lost Ball (Lift the Flap)</td></tr>
<tr><td>Kipper's Book of Colors</td><td>Kipper's Rainy Day (Lift the Flap)</td></tr>
<tr><td>Kipper's Book of Numbers</td><td>Kipper's Sunny Day (Lift the Flap)</td></tr>
<tr><td>Kipper's Book of Opposites</td><td>Kipper's Tree House (Lift the Flap)</td></tr>
</table>

Little Kippers

<table>
<tr><td>Arnold</td><td>Rocket</td></tr>
<tr><td>Butterfly</td><td>Sandcastle</td></tr>
<tr><td>Hissss!</td><td>Skates</td></tr>
<tr><td>Honk!</td><td>Splosh!</td></tr>
<tr><td>Meow!</td><td>Swing!</td></tr>
<tr><td>Picnic</td><td>Thing!</td></tr>
</table>

www.HarcourtBooks.com

First published in Great Britain in 1999 by Hodder and Stoughton Children's Books,
a division of Hodder and Stoughton Ltd.
First Red Wagon Books edition 2001

Red Wagon Books is a trademark of Harcourt, Inc., registered in the
United States of America and/or other jurisdictions.

The Library of Congress has cataloged the hardcover edition as follows:
Inkpen, Mick.
Kipper and Roly/written and illustrated by Mick Inkpen.
p.   cm.
Summary: Kipper buys a hamster as a birthday present for Pig, but he grows
to love the hamster so much that he does not want to give it away.
[1. Dogs—Fiction.   2. Hamsters—Fiction.   3. Pigs—Fiction.   4. Pets—Fiction.
5. Birthdays—Fiction.   6. Gifts—Fiction.]   I. Title.
PZ7.I564Kie   2001
[E]—dc21   00-11735
ISBN 0-15-216344-1
ISBN 0-15-204600-3 pb

A C E G H F D B

Kipper and Roly

Mick Inkpen

Red Wagon Books
Harcourt, Inc.

Orlando   Austin   New York   San Diego   Toronto   London

Pig was writing the invitations to his birthday party.

This was his wish list.

1. A pet. Like a rabbit, or a guinea pig, or something.

2. A little mouse or a gerbil.

3. Anything else.

(But mostly I would like number 1 or number 2.)

He put the names on the envelopes, and wondered what kind of pet he would get.

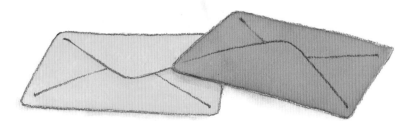

When Kipper's invitation arrived, he read it and rushed off to the pet shop to choose a pet for Pig.

The rabbit? Too sleepy.

The guinea pigs? Too timid.

The mouse? Too shy.

The stick insect? Too much like a stick. Boring.

But the hamster? The hamster was
not sleepy, or timid, or shy,
and it wasn't like
a stick at all!

It was perfect.

"One of these, please!" said Kipper.

At home Kipper gave the
hamster some sunflower seeds.
It stuffed them into its cheeks.

"Are you always this hungry?"
said Kipper.

The hamster ran up Kipper's arm
and sat on his shoulder, cleaning its
whiskers. Then it ran down the other
arm and rolled across the table.

"You can do a roly-poly!"
said Kipper. "You're so clever!"

The hamster
did it again.

The morning of the party, Roly Poly woke Kipper by nibbling on his ear.

"I wish I didn't have to give you to Pig today," said Kipper.

At breakfast Kipper began to think that maybe he would keep Roly and buy a rabbit for Pig instead.

"No. He'd like you better," sighed Kipper. "Come on. Let's wrap up your cage."

Kipper got out some scissors
and some tape, and unrolled a roll
of wrapping paper.

Roly ran into the cardboard
tube and popped out at the other
end, making Kipper giggle. Then
he slid all the way down the tube
and rolled across the floor, making
Kipper giggle again.

It gave Kipper an idea.

A big idea.

This was Kipper's big idea. It took him ages. But it worked perfectly!

"You're the best birthday present ever!" said Kipper, as Roly dropped into his paws. It was then that he remembered Pig's party!

Kipper rushed off to Pig's house. Halfway there he met Jake and Tiger, coming the other way.

"Where were you?" said Tiger. "The party's over!" But Kipper wasn't listening. He was thinking about Roly Poly.

"I can't stop!" he said. "I don't think he likes it in there very much."

Jake and Tiger began to giggle.

"Oh no! Not another one!" said Tiger.

"I'm sorry I'm late!" said Kipper as Pig opened the door. "I was playing with your present! He's brilliant, isn't he?"

Then he noticed that Pig was holding a rabbit and two guinea pigs. There was a mouse on his head and a stick insect perched on his ear.

"What are those?" said Kipper.

"They're my presents," said Pig.

They sat down at Pig's table.
Kipper fed Roly pieces of
leftover birthday cake.

"So he's not really
what you wanted?"
said Kipper.
"He's exactly
what I wanted,"
said Pig, "before
I had all these."
He pointed at his other pets.
"But it's my own fault. I should
have thought of something else to
put on my wish list."

Kipper took a big bite of cake
for himself.

"He's very nice though, isn't he?"
said Kipper. "His name is Roly Poly.
Because he can do roly-polies.
He's really good at them! And he's
always hungry. He keeps his food
in his cheeks! Look!"

Pig looked at Roly's little
fat face. It was his
turn to have
an idea.

"Kipper," said Pig, "would you do me a favor? Would you take care of Roly for me?"

Kipper was so surprised he almost choked on his cake.

"What? Take him home, you mean?" said Kipper.

Pig nodded.

"You mean he'd still be yours, but I'd take care of him?"

Pig nodded again.

"OH YES!"

said Kipper.

He said it so loudly that all
of Pig's pets jumped off the table
and hid underneath.

Kipper picked up Roly Poly,
sat him back down, and fed him
another piece of cake. Roly Poly
stopped eating for a second,
hiccuped …

. . . and started eating again.

Now Available!

At a Retailer Near You